The
Amazing Adventures of
Billy Burro

Dedicated to my precious and ever inspiring children,
Abel and Ana Maria.

Contents

CHAPTER 1

Blackpool

Villiam was a donkey who had lived in Blackpool all his life and when he grew up he married a beautiful donkey called Dorothy who he affectionately called Dottie. William and Dottie worked hard all their lives giving donkey rides to children who had come to Blackpool with their families for their summer holidays. Children of all ages enjoyed the thrill of a ride along the town's famous Golden Mile beach.

It was a hard life for William and Dottie, starting early in the morning and not getting back to their stable until late evening. In the height of the season they would work seven days a week.

However, their good nature meant that they enjoyed all the happiness and pleasure that they gave to the children when they came to visit them on the beach and especially when they were included in the children's family photographs or better still given a treat of an apple or a carrot.

William was a wise donkey and he had been careful with his money and when they were paid every week, he had put aside some of the money in a local bank. One day he planned to retire with Dottie and she had always said that she would love to go and live somewhere where it was warm and sunny for most of the year. William also thought that it would be a great opportunity for their son Billy to start a new life in a new country where the opportunities might be better because the English summer could be unpredictable. After all, who would want to go for a donkey ride if it was raining?

One evening after work William was talking with Dottie and decided it was time to mention the possibility of them moving away from Blackpool to a country where the sun was warm and fresh vegetables and fruit grew in abundance. Dottie was very excited when William mentioned that he had been saving money to pay for their retirement. William further explained that he had been speaking with a man on the phone called Pedro who lived in a little town called Mijas in southern Spain. He explained that Pedro employed donkeys who gave rides to children around this beautiful little village nestled in the mountains in a region called the Costa del Sol, or the 'coast of the sun'. William suggested to Dottie that now was time for their dreams to become reality and that the move would also make a terrific opportunity for their son Billy.

CHAPTER 2

Leaving Blackpool

Since deciding to leave Blackpool and start a new life in Mijas, William and Dottie had been very busy tidying up the stable that had been home for most of their lives.

They had only just told Billy of the journey ahead of them and as yet he had not shown any real reaction to his mum and dad's plans as he really wasn't sure of what there was in the big wide world. All he knew was the stable where they lived and the beach where he would spend many hours watching his mum and dad provide the children with their rides up and down the long flat golden sands.

It was one cold, windy and rainy morning that Dottie woke up Billy and told him to get ready for their journey. They packed what possessions they had – including their blankets and a few toys of Billy's – in the saddle bags, all neatly strapped onto their backs.

Then as John, the man who owned the stables, arrived to open the door, they all suddenly realised that the moment of the start of their journey had arrived. Billy had been told that they would be heading south for the sun, but as he looked up at the sky that morning, which was very dark grey

3

and very overcast, he didn't really know where the sun was. But he knew that his dad and mum would always continue to look after him and would make sure that they would do everything possible to achieve their dreams.

They were all suddenly sad and quite tearful as they said their goodbyes to John and he thanked William and Dorothy for all the hard work they had done for him over many years of loyal service.

Soon the three of them walked down the lane away from the farm, with Billy walking closely behind his father who headed them in the direction of Blackpool town and for the train station which was located right in the centre.

All three of them were now walking down streets where they had never been before and thankfully John had given to William some very good directions so that they knew when to turn to the left or to the right or to continue straight on. They knew that they were getting closer to the station as there were more people and cars and lorries on the roads and generally things were getting busier and busier. And soon in front of them was a large brick building with a glass-curved roof, which on the front had big letters spelling out *Welcome to Blackpool Station*.

The three entered the station and a nice young man came across to them to see if they would like some help.

'Yes please,' said William. 'Here we have some tickets to travel on the next train down to London via Manchester.'

The young man, who was called Chris, examined the tickets and said that they should head towards platform number four, which meant going down the stairs in front of them and then turning to the left and then taking the second right and up the stairs which would take them directly onto platform four. William guided his family as the guard had suggested and soon, as they walked up the stairs, there in front of them was a long train with lots of carriages painted red and blue with shiny windows. At the very end of the train there was a tiny wooden carriage.

The guard who was on the train came over to them and, having inspected the tickets, led them towards the very end of the train and to the little wooden carriage, which Billy thought looked quite cosy. The guard introduced himself as Brian and said that he would ensure that they would all have a safe and pleasant journey all the way down to London and that if they had any problems that they should come and ask for him at any time. As they got to the carriage Brian carefully opened the door that hinged down onto the platform to make a ramp for them all to walk onto. Billy and his mum and dad gently made their way into the carriage where Brian had made a nice resting area using lots of straw. In addition, he had put down some blankets just in case they got cold during the journey. There were also some carrots, a bucket of oats and plenty of fresh water.

William and Dorothy lay down next to each other on the floor of the carriage, which they found very comfortable. Billy however was far too excited and found a little opening in the side wall so he could poke his head out and have a good view of what was going on all around. This, he decided, would be his lookout as the train commenced its journey.

As Brian closed the door and made sure that everything was safe and secure, he let the family know that when they heard a whistle, which should be in about two or three minutes' time, that would be the sign that the train would be about to set off. How very exciting, thought Billy.

And a short while later, just as Brian had explained, there came the peeping sound of the whistle and a few seconds later the carriage started to shake as it jolted and they could sense that they were starting to move forward. This was a very strange sensation for them as they had never been on a train or indeed any kind of vehicle before. 'Cool!' said Billy to his mum and dad.

Billy could not believe how thrilled and excited he was to be having such a journey of a lifetime and looked across to his mum and dad, his expression wordlessly showing a big thank-you. His mum and dad looked back to acknowledge his appreciation of what they were doing for him.

Soon all the brick buildings and all the hustle and the bustle of the town were gradually replaced with large flat areas of green land where Billy saw lots of animals in the fields, some of which his father explained where moo-cows whilst the other smaller woolly animals were baa-baa-sheep. Billy's eyes looked left and right with much excitement and he was determined not to miss a thing as this wonderful journey continued. The force of the wind blowing on his face was invigorating and made him certain that this was real and not just a dream.

The carriage gently rocked from left to right and made a lovely sound as the wheels travelled over the rails, saying 'click-ity click, click-ity click, click-ity click.' The sound and the movement was very soothing and soon all three had settled down together on the straw-covered floor and fallen into a deep sleep.

As they arrived at the next station and the train had come to a halt, the big door to the carriage was gently opened and there was the smiling face of Brian to greet them. He welcomed them to Manchester station and said that they were able to get out and have a walk around and stretch their legs for ten minutes and that he would provide some fresh water and food for the next part of the journey down to London. As they wandered down onto the platform and stretched and yawned, they all decided that Brian was indeed a very kind and caring man.

Sometime later, Brian came back to tell them that the

train would shortly be departing and that they should get back into the carriage. As they got on board Brian made sure that everyone was safe and secure and then as he left the carriage he gently closed the door and fastened the lock on the outside. A while later they heard the whistle peeping to let them know that they would soon be setting off for London, the home of the Queen of England.

Click-ity click, click-ity click, click-ity click, and off they went speeding across the open countryside with Billy poking his nose out of the little opening in the side of the carriage, determined to catch all the views. This time the train seemed to go faster and faster as the green fields and valleys and the small animals in them whizzed by. At times there were big lakes to be seen and at other times the train went across bridges where busy and flowing rivers could be seen below. It was all simply marvellous in the eyes of this little donkey. The whole world, it seemed, was starting to open its doors for him.

As Billy looked in front of the train and up at the sky he could see that the clouds were starting to disappear and soon he could feel the soothing warmth of the sun on his face. How wonderful, he thought as they continued to head in the direction of the sun.

The gentle and repetitive motion of the carriage, the sounds all around them and the cosiness of the carriage made them all feel very much at peace and drowsy and soon the family was asleep once again on the straw as the train sped south to London.

CHAPTER 3

Time to see the Queen

They were all woken as the sounds around them changed. The train was slowing down and as Billy looked out of his little spy hole he could see that they were entering a big, big city. His dad told him that they were arriving in London.

Soon the train entered a large station where there were lots of platforms, and people walking around carrying bags or pushing trolleys laden with bags. Billy's father explained that they had arrived at one of London's stations, called Euston.

The little carriage came to a halt and a few moments later the sound of the lock being unfastened could be heard, and then the smiling face of Gary was there to greet them. 'Welcome to London,' he said. 'Follow me and I will show you the quickest way out so that you can continue with your journey.'

William's father lead the way followed by Dottie, then Billy at the end of the line, using his teeth to gently hold onto his mother's tail to ensure that he did not get separated. London was a very exciting place for a little donkey but at the same time it could also be very dangerous for him, and the last thing he wanted to do was to get lost.

Soon they had arrived at the exit of the station building, where Gary wished them the best of luck for the rest of their journey down to Spain. Billy's father explained to Gary that they were staying in a small block of stables for the night, just next to Saint Pancras station, where they would be catching the train the following morning to take them on their onward journey to Spain.

The streets of London were very crowded indeed and Billy could never have imagined having seen so many cars and buses and wagons and so many people all going about their business in all directions; queueing and rushing here and there and generally making everything look very, very busy. He made sure that he hung onto his mother's tail very securely but made sure he didn't bite, otherwise Mummy would not be very happy!

His father led them carefully through the streets, turning left here and then right. It seemed quite impossible for little Billy to know where they were going but soon they turned down into a very quiet lane and next to it was a large building which looked similar to the stations that Billy had seen before, only much, much bigger and grander. How exciting, he thought.

A few minutes later they made their way into the entrance of the stables where there were other horses staying but no donkeys to be seen. The man in charge of the stables checked the reservation and quickly led them to their home for the night. It was quite a small stable but it was clean and cosy.

William explained to Dottie and Billy that he had a special treat in store for them that afternoon and that there was somebody very important for them to see whilst they were staying just for the one night in London. How very mysterious and intriguing, thought Billy, who could not wait to go and explore. Having had a bite to eat and a drink of water, William led his family out onto the street to join the busy roads and avenues of London city. Soon they entered a very long and straight avenue which was lined with beautiful tall green trees with a huge park to the left which had a big lake full of ducks and geese and swans. Billy could not even take the time to blink his eyes in case he missed something!

Then Billy's father told them to look ahead and there in front of them was an enormous palace where Billy's father explained was the home of Her Majesty Elizabeth, the Queen of England. Billy could not believe that this was actually taking place. Soon the three of them were standing in front of some tall black iron railings looking at this beautiful palace. There were hundreds of people around them taking photos. As they were the only donkeys to be seen, many of the tourists also delighted in taking pictures of Billy and his mum and dad in front of the building, which his father explained was called Buckingham Palace.

Soon, to Billy's surprise, the noise of the crowds gathered in front of the palace grew louder and louder until there was a huge round of applause from everyone. As he looked around to the front he noticed that the doors to a large balcony were opening and that a beautiful lady in a gorgeous yellow dress and matching hat had come out onto the balcony and started to smile and wave at the crowd below. Billy's father explained that she was the Queen of England, our beloved Elizabeth the Second.

Billy looked up in awe at the sight of the Queen and her family on the balcony and then quite amazingly he noticed that the Queen was looking straight at him. The crowd cheered with delight as the Queen waved directly at the three donkeys standing in front of the railings as if to say, 'Thank you, my dear friends, for coming to see me today.' At this point the donkeys became famous in the eyes of the crowd and many more people came to take their photographs as they stood in front of Buckingham Palace. What a day, Billy thought. A day that he would never, ever forget.

As they made their way back to the stables, Billy looked up at the evening sky which was blue with a few cotton-wool clouds slowly drifting by. The sun was still shining and he could feel its heat keeping his back nice and warm. This was only the first day of his travels and yet his old life in Blackpool seemed very distant indeed.

CHAPTER 4

Farewell England

Billy was awoken early the next morning by his mum and dad who were tidying up the stable and packing their few belongings into their saddlebags. They said their thank-yous and goodbyes to the man in charge of the stables and within five minutes the family entered the hustle and bustle of Saint Pancras station. William showed his tickets to one of the train guards who directed him to the Eurostar section of the station where they would catch the next train to Paris. A station guard called Gregory came up to his father and directed him towards the platform where their train was stood. Billy marvelled at the train which was very long and sleek and this time to their surprise they would be staying in one of the same carriages as all the people who would be travelling on the train. This was all so very posh and fancy, marvelled Billy.

Gregory the guard showed them into their compartment, which was at the very back of the train. The room was quite small and narrow but still cosy and comfortable. As they got on board Billy looked round quickly and was delighted to see that there was an window that opened, through which he could still poke his nose so that he could see the land flying by as the magical journey continued.

It didn't seem long before the train started to shift forward. The movement of this train was far more gentle than the other train and was quieter, even though they seemed to be travelling at a faster speed. The three donkeys felt very safe and secure.

Billy poked his nose out of the window from time to time to see the beautiful English countryside of green fields and woodland flying by. This train was indeed travelling faster than the other one they had taken from Blackpool.

It didn't seem too long before the train appeared to be slowing down again, although Billy's father explained that they still had some time to go before they would arrive in Paris. Billy noticed that the train was starting to go down a long, steady slope and instead of a view of the countryside there was now a large barrier and a concrete wall coming closer to the side of the train carriage in which they were travelling. Then in an instant all the light of the day disappeared and they were travelling in almost complete darkness.

'Where has the day gone?' Billy asked his father.

William explained that they were travelling under the sea that divides England and France and that the tunnel that they were now in was known as the Channel Tunnel.

It was a strange experience for Billy as he looked out the window. He could sense that they were still moving forward but not being able to see anything outside, made it all a little confusing. However, whilst he was close to his mother and father he felt very safe indeed.

It didn't seem too long that Billy had noticed that the train was starting to go faster and faster and also seemed to be going up a slight hill. Then he noticed more and more light outside as though the sun was rising and then all of a sudden they were back out into the open countryside. 'Yippee!' he shouted.

Billy could not believe that they were now in a different country and that England was now all that way behind them. It seemed so difficult to believe that all of this could be happening to this little donkey from Blackpool.

The train continued to speed on across the flat open countryside of France. Billy started to feel quite tired and soon settled down in between Mum and Dad to enjoy the remainder of his train journey that day in the land of peace and happy dreams.

Billy and his family were awoken by the sound of the carriage door opening, and there was the happy face of Gregory the guard who had accompanied them all the way from London.

'Bienvenue à Paris,' he said to them, which Billy soon realised meant 'Welcome to Paris'.

It was just a little after midday as they entered the little stable block that had been organised for them and which thankfully was only a few minutes' walk away from the train station.

That evening the three donkeys had a splendid walk around Paris and to finish off the evening Billy's father had arranged for them to travel in a beautiful horse-drawn carriage where the sights of Paris were enjoyed to the full. Towards the end of the journey the driver of the carriage pulled up in front of a beautiful illuminated building known as the Eiffel Tower and there Billy and his mum and dad enjoyed some gorgeous pancakes known as crêpes, which were filled with a beautiful vanilla cream. How delicious, thought Billy, and what a gorgeous end to a most fantastical day.

By the time the carriage had returned the family to their stables for the night, little Billy was already fast asleep and had to be carried by his dad the last step of the journey from the carriage to his bed of straw. All of this excitement had just been too much for the little donkey, who was again in the land of dreams and peace.

CHAPTER 5

Welcome to Spain

All of the excitement and the travelling of the previous day meant that Billy had had a very good night's sleep and for once he was the first to wake. It took him a few minutes to realise exactly where he was as he was initially expecting to see the view from his old stable in dear Blackpool. It quickly dawned on him that he was now in Paris although it was still hard to believe how much had happened in such a short period of time.

After having had some carrots and oats for breakfast, the family of three made their way to the nearby train station. Once inside, a station guard called Pierre examined their tickets and led them along various corridors and onto platform number seven where the train for Malaga via Madrid stood waiting for them.

Pierre showed them to the carriage, which as usual was at the back of the train. Billy was pleased to see that there was a little peephole just big enough for him to pop his head out. He really enjoyed being at the back of the train as it gave him the opportunity to look back where the train had come from and gave him a true feeling of just how far their journey to the south was taking them. Unlike the other trains, their carriage not only had the door to lead them to the platform but also a small internal door. This, Pierre explained, would permit the guard to bring them food and drink whilst the train was still moving as the journey to Malaga would take many, many hours.

The train seemed a little older than the one they had taken to get them to Paris but nonetheless the space in their carriage was larger than on previous occasions and inside it was very comfy. Billy's father explained that the journey would take nearly two days to complete. This seemed an incredibly long period of time to Billy and really impressed upon him just how far they were travelling. His other world in Blackpool had all revolved around the same fifteen-minute walk from the stable to the beach. How things had changed for this little donkey.

Billy was becoming very used to travelling by train and he lay down next to his mother and father and smiled quite contentedly, having now got used to the rocking of the carriage and the clickity-clack clickity-clack, clickity-clack sound of the train's wheels on the tracks below.

Billy had fallen asleep but was awoken sometime later owing to the fact that the train had slowed down. He popped his head out of the opening to see that the train was starting to climb upwards towards a very hilly and moun-tainous part of the countryside which was lined on either side with beautiful green trees shaped like long brushes. His father explained that they were called pine trees. Every so often there were little torrents of water gushing and bubbling across rocky stream beds and in some areas water could be seen cascading down as waterfalls, with millions of water drops becoming as sparkly as diamonds when caught in the sunlight. On the mountains ahead of the train Billy could see that the peaks were covered in snow and certainly the air was getting colder. Were they heading back to Blackpool? he joked to himself. Once they had reached the highest part of the mountain, the train started to go down the other side. At this point Dad explained that they were now heading into Spain. At the mention of this Billy's heart raced even faster as he thought about what adventures lay ahead of him. Where would he and his mum and dad be living, and what new friends would he make?

As they headed downwards, Billy realised that the train had picked up speed on its way towards the sun. Indeed, the air outside smelt wonderful and certainly warmer than when they had left England and especially Blackpool. The train continued to go faster and faster and the mountains could now be seen only from behind.

The new land they were travelling through was quite different to anything Billy had seen before and certainly looked dryer and not as green as at home, even during the summer. There were huge planes of land with lines of straight bushy trees which looked like armies of soldiers advancing across the fields. Dad explained that these were olive trees which were farmed extensively in Spain to produce wonderful golden oil, which was tasty to eat with vegetables and good for your health. How wonderful, thought Billy.

The air smelt fresh and warm and dry in the nose of the little donkey as he continued to look south towards the front of the train. The incredible passion of his mother and father, he realised, was now starting to become a splendid reality.

18

He marvelled at his parents' bravery for actually taking the leap of faith to make their dream a reality. He vowed that he would never let them down and that each day would be treated as a very special gift. He lay in the straw next to his mum and dad and soon the happiness within sent him into the land of dreams and adventure.

Billy could not recall for how long he had been asleep but when he did wake up it felt as though it had been for quite some time as he felt very drowsy and confused as to where he was. He looked across to see his mother and father who were also sleeping. At that moment one of the guards came into the compartment from the internal door. The young man explained in quite a strange accent that he was called Manuel and that he had brought them some more food and some fresh water. He also announced that they would be arriving in Malaga in around one hour from now. The sound of the guard entering the carriage awoke Billy's mother and father. Everyone was very glad to have some fresh, cool water and some lovely apples and carrots to eat as their train journey gradually came to its end. Billy rested his nose on the opening in the carriage and soaked in the beautiful warmth of the air and the sight of the sun blazing onto the land. Now he realised why they called this area the coast of the sun.

CHAPTER 6

Billy Arrives in Malaga

The train was now travelling along land that was very flat and they were moving very fast indeed. William and Dorothy smiled at Billy, always amused at how many hours of the journey their son had spent with his head resting on the small opening of the carriage – Billy's spy hole! They were so pleased to see Billy so excited and thrilled to be travelling to their new home and to a land of immense opportunity. They realised that this bright little donkey had so much to achieve in his life and at the same time would make many others happy.

Soon the train started to slowdown and the family realised that they were now reaching the final part of their journey. Outside, they saw the views of pretty white buildings with orange-tiled roofs nestled below the beautiful cloudless blue sky. This must be Malaga. The air was fresh and warm and as William looked across at his wife, he immediately realised that he had also made his wife's dream come true.

The train finally came to a stop in what appeared to be a small and friendly station where people were not rushing around but rather taking their time and enjoying their daily lives.

Manuel, the guard, opened the outer door to the carriage and led them gently onto the platform. He pointed them in the direction of the exit, or 'salida' as it was known in Spanish. Everything around them was strange and new, but at the same time it had a friendly atmosphere and all of them felt very much at home. As they walked through the exit gate they noticed ahead of them a small thin man with long, dark brown hair who was wearing a white shirt and a straw hat. He walked towards them with an ever-increasing smile and announced that his name was Pedro ... Pedro Castillo Blanco. He was the man William had previously spoken to on the phone in Blackpool. With great joy, William introduced his wife and his son to Pedro. Upon hearing that the little donkey was called Billy, Pedro immediately said to him that as the Spanish word for donkey was 'burro', from now on his new name would be Billy Burro!

Billy was immediately taken by the friendliness of Pedro and especially by his new name, Billy Burro. Feeling an uncontrolled rush of excitement, he suddenly started to dance and jump up and down, clicking his hooves together to the delight and amazement of the passers-by in the station. The burro had arrived!

CHAPTER 7

A Short Drive to Mijas

Pedro was truly thrilled at the arrival of his new friends from England – especially Billy. He could somehow sense that this little fellow would achieve some quite remarkable things.

He led them out of the station, onto a quiet backstreet and towards an old truck which was covered in patches of rust and which he explained had once been green and white, but that, he explained, had been many years ago. Having lowered the rear tailgate of the truck, he carefully led the three donkeys into the back, Dottie first, and closed the gate securely. Making sure that everyone inside was safe, he then climbed slowly into the cab and started the engine. At first it seemed that the engine wanted to have more rest that day, but Pedro quite calmly continued trying to start it until eventually after a few minutes the sound of *put-put-put-put-put-put-put-put-put-put-put* could be heard as the motor coughed and spluttered its way into life. The vehicle lurched forward and soon the friends were on their way down the road along the coast of the sun heading in the direction of their new home in Mijas.

As the truck trundled along the busy main road Billy was able to look out through the gaps in between the wooden slats to the sides and the rear. To the left he could see the glinting and glimmering azure of the deep blue Mediterranean Sea and to the right, the beautiful pine-tree lined mountains and above a cloudless blue sky. His mum and dad appeared equally excited as all three took in the new scenery with not a word needing to be said. They were all truly speechless.

A short while later, Pedro turned the truck off the main road and it slowed down as it started to pull up the hill, winding up to the left and then to the right. It seemed as though they were driving along the back of a snake, thought Billy.

Clearly they were heading up into the mountains. Then in front of them, nestled in the hillside, was a beautiful village with amazing white cottages with quaint orange-topped roofs all nestled in amongst the pine tree forests. At the very top was a beautiful church bell tower. Soon they entered the town and passed the shops and offices and cafés, soon noticing the happy smiling faces of the people. In the background the church bell rang to signal the arrival of midday … ding-dong … ding-dong … ding-dong … or were the bells hailing the arrival of Billy?

Pedro drove the truck through the main square of the village and then, after a short distance of more driving up into the hills, he pulled up the wagon outside a small barn with a quaint little cottage to the side. Pedro called out to his wife Juanita and his children Ana Maria and Abel. All came out of the house to welcome the new arrivals from England with open arms, smiles of joy and shouts of delight. Pedro jumped out of his truck to hug his wife and children and then unfastened the rear door. The children ran into the truck to put their arms around the donkeys. Seeing the smaller one, they gave him an extra long hug and kiss. Billy was overwhelmed.

The family of donkeys stood motionless and speechless, trying to take in all the joy and happiness they were experiencing as they looked around at their new home. They gave their thanks to God for this truly great blessing and wondrous opportunity.

Pedro and his family led William, Dorothy and Billy to their stable block which had a lovely paddock all kept cool under the shade of the welcoming fronds of a large and ancient palm tree.

It would, Billy thought, take quite some time to fully absorb all that was going on. His life, it seemed, had completely changed.

They stood in silence, feeling the warmth of the afternoon sun and the freshness of the cool mountain breeze and the tranquillity of all that surrounded them. His first day in Mijas he would certainly never forget.

CHAPTER 8

Billy's First Morning in Mijas

The sound of the breeze gently humming through the trees and the warmth of the early morning sun gently woke Billy from his night's deep sleep. He knew he had slept well as he awoke in a very calm and happy mood. He looked over at his mum and dad. They were sleeping side by side with their heads touching. What happiness this little village created, Billy thought.

He had had enough sleep and decided that the streets and patios were to be explored whilst it was still so quiet and before his breakfast would be ready.

Gently he made his way out of the paddock and set off as quietly as he could down the stone path that meandered its way down to sleepy Mijas.

Soon the path turned to tarmac and he found himself at the entrance to a large square, with a bubbling fountain in the middle. He set off down one of the side streets which had stone cobbles and was quite narrow. He thought how strange and yet how wonderful that already he felt so much at home here. On he went, not knowing where to go when he came to a junction – left or right or straight on, what did it matter? He realised that he could never feel lost or scared in his new home.

The path he was on led gently upwards and he noticed that he was getting nearer to the beautiful church tower he had briefly seen yesterday as Pedro drove the truck up the hill into the village. Just to the right of the church tower was a rather strange-looking building that puzzled him. It had tall walls, painted white, that seemed to be curved all the way round such that the building was, he imagined, completely circular, and yet there was no roof to be seen.

As he approached the building he decided he would follow the curved wall and headed around the left-hand side. Round it went, perfectly curved and perfectly white. And then, even though it was so early in the morning and he had not yet seen a soul moving, he came across someone. It was, he thought, like a little moo-cow except that it was a boy. Was this a bull? he thought. The animal was quite small and had a beautiful black gleaming coat and a rugged and very handsome face and a pair of ivory horns. Its legs looked very powerful and its body very lean and strong, and very broad. Billy approached the little fellow gently and from the somewhat sad look on its face it seemed as if the little chap had been stood here next to the door of the strange round building for quite some time. Indeed, as Billy moved closer the little fellow didn't even bother to look up, despite the fact that he must have heard Billy's hooves clip-clopping towards him.

Finally the little bull looked up and stared at Billy, quite surprised to see anyone at this time of day. Billy said hello and asked if he could help in any way.

The little bull was silent and dropped his head down to look at the ground again. Then sensing that Billy was still there and seemingly waiting for a reply, he explained what had happened.

The little bull had been brought a long distance to the village by his owner and up to the big round building which his owner had explained was a special place where bulls were put into a large ring to entertain a large crowd of people. How the bull was to entertain the crowd his owner had not explained. Then it appeared that the owners of the building had refused to allow the little bull into the ring. He had heard them say, 'He is too young.' And so the owners had left feeling disappointed and annoyed and had even left the little bull behind. It seemed, the little bull explained, that nobody wanted him. He had spent the whole night tied up against the building. He explained to Billy that he was tired and hungry but very glad that Billy had stopped and talked to him. Suddenly a warm smile appeared on the little bull's face.

Billy quickly realised that the little fellow had no home to go to and decided that he must take him back home to Pedro's ranch, sure that Pedro would be able to help.

Billy nibbled on the rope that tethered the little bull to the side of the building and in no time at all the rope became frayed and eventually Billy's teeth cut all the way through.

'Little bull,' he said, 'you are free. Please trust me and follow me.'

As Billy turned around to lead the way back to where he had come from, he initially heard nothing behind him. And then as he kept on walking, he joyfully heard the sound of the bull's hooves on the stone cobbles as he started to follow behind.

As they arrived at the main square, Billy stopped and turned around to face his new friend. You are indeed a very special creature and very brave, he thought, for having spent the whole night all on his own and not knowing what would happen to you. He explained to the little bull that his name was Billy Burro and as he looked at his little friend he chuckled and thought that this courageous little chap could perhaps be called Bravo the Bull. When he said this out loud, the little bull immediately warmed to Billy's suggestion.

'Bravo the Bull it is,' said the bull, suddenly looking proud and happy and standing tall as one would expect of such a magnificent and splendid animal.

The two walked side by side up the gravel track leading to Pedro's farm. As they arrived at the paddock, Pedro was already busy cleaning out the stable block and providing fresh water and food. He beamed a huge smile as he saw Billy walking towards him with the beautiful black bull with its rugged face and gleaming horns.

Billy explained the whole storey to Pedro and felt so happy when he saw Pedro take Bravo to the adjoining stable, where he was given food and water and a bed of straw to lie down upon.

How wonderful it's been already, and all before my first Mijas breakfast, thought Billy as he watched his new friend tuck heartily into his morning meal.

CHAPTER 9

The New Friends Start their New Adventures

It was Monday morning and the start of Billy's second day in Mijas and his first day of work.

Pedro arrived to provide breakfast, and as a special treat in amongst the oats was also included some chopped carrot and apples. Hmm, very tasty, thought Billy as he tucked in and smiled lovingly across to his mum and dad, who Pedro explained were having a lie-in – and clearly enjoying it, judging by the sound of all the snoring, thought Billy.

Pedro explained that he would be taking Billy down to the stand that he had in the village centre where families would be waiting to have their donkey rides around the village. For young Billy it was a moment of great excitement and he was sure that all the training he had received from Dottie and William in Blackpool would now be put to good use. He was determined that he would not let them down and would certainly do the best job he could for Pedro in view of the wonderful opportunity this kind man of Spain had given him and his parents.

Bravo was still sleeping in his stable and no doubt still feeling tired from his travels and his ordeal of having been left outside the big white round building all night.

Pedro led two other donkeys out of their stable and introduced brothers Juan and Julio to Billy.

'Mucho gusto,' they said together as they rubbed noses with the new boy from England.

Billy was thrilled and replied, 'Encantado,' as he had learned a few words of Spanish already.

Soon they were down at the stand, where they were given their beautiful uniforms to wear. Pedro placed a fine, soft sheepskin blanket over Billy's back and then placed a small leather saddle on top gently fastening the strap around his tummy. With a leather rein and harness Billy felt that he was ready for action. He had a sudden vision of his mum and dad ready for work on Blackpool beach. Finally Pedro appeared out of the store room with a straw hat with a large hole on either side which he placed onto the young donkey's, head feeding his long brown ears through the holes. How thrilling, Billy thought. He was now ready for work and to prove to all that he could continue the family tradition.

It was still early and yet families were already arriving and children's faces were looking very excited at the thought of being able to have a gentle ride on a donkey through the picturesque streets of Mijas.

Pedro explained to the three donkeys that Juan and Julio would take the lead with Billy behind so that he could see how the job of gently carrying the children was done and eventually so that he could learn the route to be taken through the village. Billy could not wait to get started, although he could feel that some little butterflies were starting to flutter around in his tummy!

As Billy stood behind the two brothers, Juan looked back and smiled warmly at him. Everything would be fine.

In no time, the first customers had arrived and, having paid their money to Pedro, a boy and girl used the stone mounting block to climb up onto the backs of the Juan and Julio. When the children had their feet safely in the stirrups, Pedro gently moved the two donkeys forward and suddenly it was Billy's turn. He took a few steps and stood next to the block. A little girl stood next to him and gave him a gentle stroke on his shoulder and then climbed onto the block and then sat into Billy's saddle. Billy could hardly feel her weight and soon Juan and Julio were starting to set off, with Billy following behind. How proud Billy felt on this, his first day as a working donkey and in such an unimaginable setting which had become his new home.

The pace was gentle and Billy could feel the little girl on his back gently stroking the back of his head and laughing at the thrill of the ride. Billy made sure that each step was with great care to ensure that his passenger would enjoy every step and feel safe.

The two brothers in front led Billy down quaint streets lined with terraces of beautiful white houses with their orange-tiled roofs and windows and balconies adorned with pots of vivid green and red geranium plants. The air was cool and fresh and the sun gently warming. This was indeed a paradise, Billy thought to himself. Soon they had walked up by the big circular building and then on towards the church where the bell struck ten times for ten o'clock in the morning. The sound of the bell was very calming as little Billy continued on his journey. Some minutes later and Pedro brought the three donkeys to a stop as they reached the end of a terrace high up in the village, next to another beautiful church built from within the rock. At this special place, the breeze was stronger and the air felt warmer. Then Billy looked across to the right where in the distance he saw the beautiful reflection of the sun glinting off the Mediterranean Sea as though a million stars were all winking and smiling at him. Where the sea met the shore, there was a town of white towers and houses and villas which Pedro had explained was called Fuengirola. The sight of all the scenery took Billy's breath away. He could never have imagined such beauty and such peace and happiness.

Pedro called the donkeys to walk on and the little party set off back down the narrow streets in the direction of the main square where they had started. Billy's passenger had clearly enjoyed herself and soon gave Billy a big hug to say thank you as she got down off Billy's back and onto the mounting block. Billy gave a very happy 'hee-haw' and moved his head up and down. Pedro came and gave him a big hug as confirmation that this little donkey from England was going to do his new job very well indeed.

More rides continued through the streets and Billy felt so proud that he was bringing such delight and happiness to the children. He was more thrilled to see the faces of the parents as they arrived back to the starting point knowing that the little donkey had looked after their child safely and with great and loving care.

Billy's first working day had come to an end as Pedro led the three back to the little store building just off from the main square, where he carefully removed their saddles and harnesses. A good firm rub and a pat on their backs gave Juan, Julio and Billy the assurance that Pedro was very happy with the day's work and soon they were heading back up the narrow lane to the farm.

To Billy's delight, Dottie and William were waiting at the top of the lane and trotted down eagerly to hear how their son had found his first day. How thrilled they were as Billy recounted the day's events with much glee.

Bravo the bull was also in his paddock and gave a great smile and a big snort to express his delight that his new friend Billy was back home again.

CHAPTER 10

Bravo gets a Job

Billy was so much enjoying his first days and his first week of work. Every day he felt as though he had achieved so much and brought so much happiness to the families and especially the children to whom he was giving such pleasurable rides around the village throughout the day.

It was always a delight to come back to the farm in the evening to see his mum and dad and spend the evening talking with Bravo, when he had completed his chores.

It was becoming clear to Billy that the number of children waiting in the queue for rides was getting longer and longer each day as the holiday season got busier and busier. He needed, he thought, to find a solution both to help Pedro and also to help his friend Bravo, who he could see was not too happy at spending day after day with nothing to do on Pedro's farm.

One evening after work and having completed all his chores for his mum and dad, Billy called to see Pedro at the farmhouse. He explained to Pedro that the children should not be kept waiting for too long in the queue and that they needed another donkey to help out. 'Better still,' explained the very clever little donkey from England, 'perhaps we need to provide something a little different and special to the holidaymakers.'

Pedro was all ears.

Billy continued with his suggestion. Pedro listened intently, realising that Billy had a great mind for business. Billy explained that he was sure that Bravo could also be used to provide the children with rides around the village. Pedro stood up and explained that Bravo was a bull and that nobody, but nobody, would ever ride on the back of a bull, especially children.

Pedro's son overheard this conversation and asked his father to let him try. Pedro looked at his son in amazement and then at Billy, and then realised he had no option but to put his faith in Billy's idea.

Billy went across to have a chat with Bravo to explain to him what the plan was. Bravo was delighted to hear that he was also being given the chance to work and especially delighted at the thought of doing the same kind of work that clearly brought such delight and happiness to Billy.

A few minutes later Pedro walked over to Bravo with his largest saddle and carefully placed it on the bull's back.

Pedro was clearly nervous, and Billy could see that Bravo was even more nervous. The powerful black bull stood as still as a statue while Pedro's son climbed onto the big wide animal and finally got his feet into the stirrups on either side of the saddle. His son had the confidence of Billy and was determined to make this work. Pedro motioned for Bravo to start walking forward, which he did with great gentleness and skill and much to the delight of his son and Pedro. Billy was thrilled that his faith in Bravo was well placed. After ten minutes of walking around the paddock area of the farm, Pedro looked at his wife Juanita and they both realised that what Billy had said was true. They had a new donkey to help them with their work – except the new donkey was a bull, whose previous destiny was to fight.

The following morning Billy led Bravo down the lane to the village. The sight of this fearful creature walking through the streets caused much amazement among the villagers and even more among the tourists and their children. Even the local policeman stood ready for action.

Bravo walked tall and proud but with a kind and gentle face and a soft stride as he made his way through the village streets. Soon the three donkeys and the bull all had their saddles on and stood in line by the mounting block. Within seconds, the first two children climbed onto the backs of Juan and Julio. The next in line was a brother and sister and it was the boy who quickly climbed up onto Billy's back. His sister looked up admiringly at the big black bull and walked towards him to gently rest her head on his side, listening, it seemed, to his breathing and his heartbeat. She spread her hands across his side and then with a deep breath climbed onto the mounting block and onto the saddle. Her parents looked on at the amazing braveness of this little girl. Others stood in the square, motionless and in complete silence. Billy looked behind at Bravo and nodded a 'let's go'. Then

he walked forward and gently Bravo followed on behind, walking as though he wore sheepskin-lined slippers, so gentle was his walk. He was truly a beautiful and graceful bull with great gentleness as all could see.

The little girl sat upon the back of the bull and gently rubbed his shoulders as if to say that he was doing such a great job and giving her such pleasure. Bravo continued to follow Billy through the streets, feeling as proud as anybody could feel especially upon seeing the faces of both the holidaymakers and the local residents of Mijas admiring this great sight. How many photos people were taking that morning Billy could not imagine.

Soon the ride was over as the little girl stood up off her saddle to get off the great bull and make her way safely down the mounting block. Again she pressed her head against the side of the great beast as if to say thank you and that she would see him again. Then she was off to her mum and dad to explain the thrill of the ride and to admire the photos her dad had so proudly taken. There was a round of applause and cheers of delight from all the folk in the square.

None was more amazed than Pedro whose smile of joy and disbelief was immense as he walked across to Billy to give him the biggest hug imaginable. As he had seen in his dreams, this little donkey from England truly had the gift to do some amazing and wonderful things – and today' s events were no doubt just the beginning.

CHAPTER 11

Ding-dong, Ding-dong, Ding-donk!

The two dynamic friends Billy and Bravo continued to work carefully and skilfully and to the delight of Pedro in the days and weeks to come, finding great reward in the evenings after a hard day's work. How much pleasure they continued to provide to the tourist families visiting Mijas, as well as the people who lived in this special little town.

Billy had come to love the sound of the church bells which struck on the hour throughout the daytime to let him and everybody in the town know the time of day without the need to wear a watch. It was on a Thursday just after Billy and Bravo had started working in the afternoon that Billy heard something very strange. He had previously heard the church bells ring twice for 2 o'clock in the afternoon, and at 3 o'clock the bells started again as he expected. Ding-dong, ding-dong, and finally a ding-donk. The bells had rung three times but what had happened to the last dong? This played on his mind for the rest of the afternoon and more so when at 4 o'clock just one of the two bells rang for just one long tone … dinggggg.

Back at the farm that evening Billy completed his chores and then asked his mum and dad if he could go and have a word with Pedro. Pedro explained that there had indeed been a problem with the church bells. The bells were over 100 years old and it had been discovered that afternoon that one of the bells had become cracked which explained why it could no longer ring its beautiful and familiar tone. Billy enquired of Pedro as to how long it would take to get the bell repaired. That's when Pedro explained some bad news. 'My dear Billy,' he explained, 'we have the money to have the bell taken to the foundry in Malaga where it can be repaired to make it ring as it should for many years to come. However, the problem we have is that over the years more houses have been built so close to the church tower so that it will now be difficult, if not impossible, to get a big enough lorry with a crane on the back in order to lift the bell down from the tower.' Upon hearing this news, Billy formed a plan. He went into town that evening and having arrived at the church tower looked around to see just how little space there was to get a large truck into the area just as Pedro had explained. Now he could understand the problem.

That night Billy had little sleep as his mind tried to find a solution to the problem of having the church bell taken down from the tower so that it could be fixed at the foundry.

The next day, whilst Billy and Bravo were taking their passengers around the village, Bravo noticed that Billy had a very happy and contented look on his face. When he asked his friend why such happiness Billy smiled and explained that all would be revealed after work that evening. Billy had also asked if Pedro could provide him with a long length of strong reliable rope. Pedro once again was amazed to guess at what this little donkey's mind could be thinking.

On Saturday morning Pedro led Billy and Bravo into town and Bravo noticed that the rope that had previously been discussed was being carried by Pedro. What, the little bull thought, was going on?

The three arrived at the church tower to be met by Señor Carlos, who looked after and repaired the church including making sure that its walls were kept painted beautifully white. Señor Carlos took one of the ends of the rope and started to make his way up the old narrow steps of the church tower all the way to the very top. Whilst he was doing this Billy and Pedro led Bravo down the street, walking away from the church tower, and then as Billy looked back he told Bravo to stop. Pedro started to pass the rope around the shoulders of Bravo having secured it first with a good firm knot.

Pedro then looked up at the top of the church tower and

saw that Señor Carlos was waving at him. Pedro explained to Billy that all was ready.

Billy asked Bravo to walk forwards very slowly. The bell moved upwards as the rope attached to his shoulders became tight and then Bravo stopped just for a second as the resistance of the rope continued to increase. And then he continued a few more steps until Billy heard a loud clunk from the top of the church tower and then told him to stop. Billy and Pedro looked up at the church tower to see that the damaged bell had been lifted from its timber cradle and was now being supported by the rope secured firmly around Bravo. Billy instructed Bravo to start walking backwards, slowly, slowly, slowly. Señor Carlos was now sitting on top of the bell as this was being gradually lowered down the outside of the church tower and as the bell continued moving downwards Señor Carlos used his feet to push the bell away from the wall of the tower to stop the heavy bell damaging the building. At that time a small truck with a flatbed arrived and was carefully reversed into position. Billy continued to guide Bravo, walking backwards down the path getting ever nearer and nearer to the church and allowing the bell to get closer and closer to the ground. Billy then told Bravo to stop whilst the truck was positioned directly under the bell. Bravo then continued with his final steps in reverse until the bell finally and gently settled onto the back of the truck and the rope became slack. Villagers stood in silence and in complete amazement having seen what had happened and that the bell was now safely down at ground level and ready to be driven to the foundry for repairs. Billy, looking round at the faces, realised that the true celebration could only start once the repaired bell was back home and safely installed in the tower as until then the church tower would remain silent.

It was two weeks later when Billy, Bravo and Pedro were

stood waiting outside the church tower. This time Bravo knew what was going to happen, because Pedro was carrying the same length of rope as in the previous week. The sound of the little truck could be heard squeezing its way through the narrow passageways before it eventually stopped just by the side of the church tower, as previously. The villagers had once again gathered, albeit in greater numbers than last time, to watch an historic moment unfolding before their very eyes. The rope was passed up through to the top of the church tower and back down and secured onto the ring at the top of the bell, whilst the other end was gently tied around the broad and powerful shoulders of Bravo.

'Forward, my friend,' said Billy as Bravo started to gently walk up the lane. As the rope became tight Señor Carlos climbed up onto the top of the bell as it gradually started its upwards journey. Gently it climbed against the wall of the church tower with the guiding feet of Señor Carlos preventing the bell from causing damage to the old stone walls of the beautiful church. Up the lane continued Billy and Bravo with the great bull hardly feeling any weight as he continued with his steps. Eventually Billy told Bravo to stop and then to go back two steps. The familiar clunk was heard as the bell was returned home to the safety of its timber cradle. Señor Carlos waved from above that all was well and lowered the rope back down to ground level. Billy and Bravo returned to the base of the tower to look up and see the bell now back in its home no doubt for many years to come. The crowd again stared in amazement, seeing how skilfully Billy had managed the whole operation.

With only minutes to spare, it would soon be time for the three o'clock bells to ring. Everybody was silent and gazed upwards to the top of the tower when suddenly they cheered to the delight of ding-dong, ding-dong, ding-dong.

Living life to the full, thought Billy. There is no other way!!

CHAPTER 12

Jessica and Victoria head to Spain

If Billy had worked especially hard during the week, Pedro would often let him have Saturday and Sunday off as free time.

Billy had got to know Señora Moncayo who ran the small bakery in the village. The shop was located in a very old part of Mijas and access to it was only by foot as it was too narrow for any cars or lorries to get down the passageways. This created a problem for Señora Moncayo as she needed to take delivery of several sacks of flour every week in order to make her bread and cakes. Billy the ever resourceful had

43

managed to borrow a small wooden cart. With the help of Bravo, the sacks of flour were loaded onto the cart which Billy then pulled down the narrow lane all the way to the shop. This was a great help to Señora Moncayo and it gave her one less difficult job to do.

Whilst making the delivery, Señora Moncayo explained to Billy that she was holding a competition the following weekend whereby her customers were invited to bring in a special bread or cake to her shop which she would put on display in the window and sell, with the proceeds going to the local children's charity. Billy thought how wonderful it would be if he could enter the competition and suddenly thought of his Aunt Jessica, who was still living in Blackpool. His aunt had retired some years back and had been a most excellent cake maker and in particular Billy could vividly remember her Victoria sponge. As he stood there on the street saliva was dripping from his chin at the thought of biting into the soft, light sponge and tasting the buttercream and raspberry jam filling.

Having completed his chores that day, he went to his favourite telephone box and decided to make a call to Aunt Jessica. How pleased she was to hear from her favourite nephew Billy and that he was doing so well and settling into his new home in Mijas. Billy explained about the cake competition and asked whether Jessica could possibly make a cake and send it in the post to Spain.

'Dear me,' she exclaimed. 'Whilst I could certainly make you a cake, Billy, there is no way it could be sent in the post to Spain. It would get smashed to pieces!'

There was a moment's silence and then Jessica suggested to Billy why didn't she give him the recipe so that he could make the cake himself. Billy had never made a cake before but realised that there was nothing to lose from trying to do something for the first time. After all, the cake was being made in aid of the local children's charity. Details were taken down over the phone and the donkey's action plan was set in motion.

Having obtained all of the ingredients and studied the recipe Aunt Jessica had given him, Billy arranged with Pedro that he would make the cake at the farm on the Friday night so that it could be delivered freshly to Señora Moncayo's bakery on the Saturday morning in readiness for the competition. That week Billy worked very hard indeed and made sure that by Friday lunchtime he had earned Pedro so much money that he allowed him to have Friday afternoon off so that he could go back to the farm and start with the cake preparations.

Later that evening as Pedro arrived home, he chuckled in delight to see the little English donkey now appearing as a white ghost as he was covered in flour from head to tail. However, the smell of the cake in the oven was delightful, thought Pedro, and something that he had never smelt before during his entire life in Spain. Later that evening once the cake had cooled, Billy carefully prepared the buttercream filling and applied this very carefully and then added a thin layer of raspberry jam that he had managed to buy from the local shop.

The cake was finally given a dusting of powdery sugar, and how magnificent and elegant it looked. It was, after all, perhaps the first Victoria sponge in the history of Mijas and it had been made by an English donkey to boot!

The following morning Billy was up early and having carefully placed the cake in a box he then carried it down into the village on the back of his little cart all the way to Señora Moncayo's shop. How exquisite the cake looked, thought Señora Moncayo, who had no hesitation in placing the sponge right in the centre of the window display so that all the customers would be able to see it. She carefully sliced it into twenty-five equal segments planning to sell each slice for five euros to help raise as much money as possible for the children's charity.

Billy had work to do that morning and in addition had to go and collect the sacks of flour for Señora Moncayo on his little cart. By the time he had finished and returned back to the shop, the churchbell had just rung ten times. As he looked in the window there were still quite a few cakes and breads left on display but the Victoria sponge was nowhere to be seen. Señora Moncayo came running out of the shop to explain to Billy that his cake had been the most popular and had sold within thirty minutes of the shop opening with many customers requesting a whole cake be made for them for the following weekend. Billy was amazed and wondered how on earth all the extra cakes that Señora Moncayo's customers would be demanding could possibly be made.

He was back on the phone to Aunt Jessica to tell her of the great success of her cake recipe which had been the most popular and had won the competition. How pleased and delighted was Billy's aunt especially due the fact that her nephew was the one who had baked it.

As they talked further, Billy realised that his aunt was perhaps a little lonely living in Blackpool especially during the cold, dark winter months now that William and Dottie had moved away and especially Billy. Clearly she missed the company of her family and often found herself feeling lonely. How she marvelled at the determination and courage that Billy's parents had shown in deciding to leave their hometown in search of a new life in the sun. Billy felt quite concerned at his aunt's sadness and wondered what he could do to improve her situation.

Billy was aware from his earlier discussions with Señora Moncayo that she had a little stable block round the back of her shop which was currently empty.

Later that day Billy called to see Señora Moncayo to explain to her the possibility of large numbers of the Victoria sponge cakes being made – but not by him. Señora Moncayo was puzzled until Billy suggested to her that maybe she invite his Aunt Jessica to come and live with her as the little stable block to the rear of the shop was empty, and in exchange Aunt Jessica could assist with the cake making. The look of happiness on the face of Señora Moncayo was like the morning sun rising and she hugged Billy dearly realising that he had again devised a most amazing solution to help and improve the lives of others. What an inspiring and wonderful creature he was!

It was some two weeks later as Billy was pulling flour on his cart down to the bakery shop that he heard the sound of Pedro's old truck labouring up the hill into the village. He stopped and looked behind as the truck came into view and slowed to a stop. As he focused his sight, he noticed a little donkey in the back of the truck who he immediately recognised as his Aunt Jessica.

As tears ran down his cheeks in delight, he knew without a doubt that two fine old English ladies, Jessica and Victoria, had now made their new home in Mijas.

CHAPTER 13

Fruity Fellows

Another week was drawing to a close and Billy and Bravo were walking back up to the farm at the end of the day's work with Pedro. They always enjoyed these walks as Pedro would often tell them stories of his life of growing up as a little boy in Mijas. Today the two were being told of Pedro's two brothers who are called Pablo and Roberto.

Pedro explained that his two brothers had worked all their lives as farmers and that now was a busy time of the year as the crops needed to be harvested. Billy suggested to Pedro that as he and Bravo were not working this Saturday they could help down at his brothers' farms. Pedro was delighted at the suggestion and explained that they could always do with help carrying sacks of the produce.

The next morning it was Saturday and Billy and Bravo woke up early, keen to find out what they could do on the farms. Pedro had given them directions and both farms were next to each other and just fifteen minutes' walk away.

A while later they arrived at the farm to be greeted by Pablo and Roberto and some of their friends and family, who were delighted to see them, having heard so many stories of their acts of kindness in the village since their arrival.

Billy was very excited to look around Pablo's farm, which had lots and lots of trees with shiny green leaves and little tiny orange fruits, which Pablo explained were called clementines. Billy immediately knew this fruit as it was a particular favourite of his Aunt Jessica, who was known to eat a whole box of clementines in just one day. He wondered what would happen to Pablo's fruit farm if Aunt Jessica ever found out where it was!

As Pablo was explaining to Billy how the fruit was carefully removed from the tree and then placed into baskets, he suggested that Billy and Bravo assist with carrying the baskets into the barn. Billy moved up to one of the trees and gently sniffed at the nearest clementine hanging from the branch. How good it smelt, he thought. And then without realising, he put his lips around the clementine and gently pulled it away from the branch. He then carefully placed it into the basket on the ground below. Pablo watched in amazement at how gently Billy had removed the fruit and upon examining the clementine he saw that the skin had not been damaged at all. Pablo asked Billy if he could pick some more from the tree. Six more were gently removed and placed into the basket and all were perfectly intact. Billy suggested that it would be easier if the baskets could be placed onto his saddlebags as it would make it easier for him to place the fruits there as opposed to on the ground. This was arranged and Pablo and his family watched in amazement as the little donkey gradually made his way around the tree starting to fill the baskets with the beautiful orange clementines. Once the baskets were full, he walked across to the little barn where they were then placed into the shade and new baskets fixed onto his saddle. Billy then went to the next tree and the next tree and soon many baskets were being filled much to Pablo's delight. A while later Pablo asked Billy to have a break and he and Bravo enjoyed some fresh water, some clementines and some rather beautiful green olives.

Bravo in particular was very partial to olives. Pablo's brother Roberto explained that he had an olive farm right next to Pablo's farm. He let Billy and Bravo through the gate and there in front of them were hundreds and hundreds of small green trees covered with fat, shiny green olives.

Roberto explained that it was quite difficult for him and his wife to collect the olives from the trees as this required using very long sticks and beating the branches so that the olives fell down onto the ground where nets had been laid. As soon as all of the ripe olives had fallen into the net this would then be gathered up and the olives placed into wooden boxes.

Bravo saw Billy staring at him in a rather unusual way. Something's being planned, thought Bravo, and it probably involves me!

Billy walked across to Bravo and whispered into his ear and then gave him some instructions. Bravo was told to turn around so that his back was facing the olive tree nearest to them. Then Billy came alongside him and asked Bravo to reverse until Billy told him to stop. Billy checked Bravo's position in relation to the trunk of the tree and then told him to raise his right rear leg and kick backwards. The little bull was quite confused and felt a little silly with these instructions but as ever he never had any reason to doubt his dear friend. Bravo did as he was told and as his hoof struck the trunk of the tree there was a very loud thump. The whole tree shook and as it did the little ripe olives all came cascading down into the nets below. Roberto and his wife stood back in amazement at what they had just seen.

Billy positioned Bravo against the next tree and once again the great powerful bull kicked backwards with an amazing thump. Once again the little tree shook and the beautiful ripe olives all came tumbling down to the ground.

Pablo and the rest of the family and friends had wondered what the strange thumping sound was and came across to see Billy and Bravo in action. All were absolutely amazed at this new style of olive harvesting.

The two friends continued with the harvesting works and by early afternoon all of the ripe fruits from the clementine trees and the olive trees were safely in the boxes in the shade of the barn, ready to be sold at market the following day.

Later that evening Billy and Bravo were resting at home, admiring the view of the beautiful little mountain village of Mijas below them with the expanse of the glittering Mediterranean Sea as a most amazing backdrop.

Having enjoyed their day's labour as new-boy fruit farmers, both sat there with pleasant grins on their faces.

Bravo chuckled to himself as he looked across at the orange stained lips of the little English donkey and wondered what other amazing adventures Billy would have in store for them.

THE END

About the Author

Yorkshire born Greg Harris inadvertently fell into the world of insurance claim management when he left school and soon found himself travelling and living the world over, meeting and helping people of all nationalities, whose homes or businesses had been badly damaged.

He has run 9 full marathons for Children's charities and has just started performing in public with his voice and his trusted guitar.

His beloved Yorkshire is once again his home.

Greg's main philosophy is "Treat life as a continuous education."

Lightning Source UK Ltd.
Milton Keynes UK
UKHW011550161122
412294UK00002B/42